W9-BHX-691

THE GRUNT AND THE GROUCH

Beastly Feast!

STONE ARCH BOOKS
a capstone imprint

First published in the United States in 2012
by Stone Arch Books
A Capstone Imprint
1710 Roe Crest Drive
North Mankato, Minnesota 56003
www.capstonepub.com

First published by
Stripes Publishing
1 The Coda Centre, 189 Munster Road
London SW6 6AW

Library of Congress Cataloging-in-Publication Data is available on
the Library of Congress website.

ISBN: 978-1-4342-4603-5 (hardcover)
ISBN: 978-1-4342-4269-3 (paperback)

Summary: The Grunt and the Grouch get in trouble in the school
cafeteria, find the perfect pet, and visit the barbershop.

Printed in the United States of America in Stevens Point, Wisconsin.
042012   006678WZF12

THE GRUNT AND THE GROUCH

GROUCH

Beastly Feast!

Written by
TRACEY CORDEROY

Illustrated by
LEE WILDISH

THE GRUNT AND THE GROUCH

CONTENTS

Chapter 1

Rummmmble! The Grunt stuck his head into the fridge, peered around, and groaned. It was completely bare from top to bottom. They were all out of moldy cheese, slime cakes, and cockroach chips.

Grunty's tummy gave another loud rumble. He was starving.

"Grouchy!" he bellowed, his head still stuffed in the fridge. "Come here!"

The Grouch hurried into the kitchen.
"Oh, no! You're stuck!" cried the small
green troll. "Don't panic, I'll rescue you!"
    He grabbed onto Grunty's rear end
and huffed and puffed, pulling as
hard as he could.

"Get off!" The Grunt growled. "I'm not stuck!" He reached a hairy, purple arm behind his back and pushed Grouchy away. Then he backed out of the fridge.

"Why haven't you gone to the grocery store?" The Grunt bellowed.

"It was your turn," Grouchy snapped at him.

"It was not!" The Grunt argued.

"Was too!"

"Was not!"

"Was too!" cried The Grouch. "You told me last week that if I promised not to pick up my clothes and remembered not to flush the toilet, you'd do the shopping. And I didn't do either of those things. So it was your turn!"

Just then, the mail slot in the front door popped open. An envelope sailed straight through the slot and landed on the floor.

"Humph!" snorted Grunty. "I bet that's just another bill! No food in the house and a big fat bill to pay. What a day this is turning into!"

He stomped across to the front door and snatched up the letter. He was about to rip it up, when . . .

"Wait!" cried Grouchy. "Look on the back — it's us!"

The Grunt flipped the envelope over. Sure enough, someone had drawn a picture of the trollrific pair on the back! Grunty looked like a big purple scribble with green stuff dripping from his nose. And Grouchy looked like a Brussels sprout wearing a hat!

"They look just like us, don't they?" Grouchy said with a grin.

"Yeah, but who would be sending us mail?" asked The Grunt as he eagerly tore open the envelope.

Inside, they found a letter and two fancy-looking tickets. Grunty unfolded the letter and started to read.

The letter was from Nick, a boy they'd met when they'd been substitute teachers for a day at Sparkleton Elementary School, the cleanest, most spotless school in the entire world. Or at least it had been until The Grunt and

The Grouch visited. It had never been quite the same after the trolls' Rats Awards!

"Hey, listen to this!" cried Grunty. "Nick says there's a party at school this afternoon! His parents have chickenpox and can't go, so he's giving us their tickets instead. The school won some

Mr. Spickspan cordially invites you to celebrate
Sparkleton Elementary School's
Healthy Food Award.

Date and Time: July 15ᵗʰ at 3:15 p.m.
Where: Sparkleton Elementary cafeteria
Dress: Fancy

healthy food award. The mayor will be there, and there's going to be tons of food!"

The Grunt waved the silver tickets under Grouchy's nose.

"But look," groaned Grouchy, "the invitation says we have to dress fancy! And won't all the food be healthy? Yuck!"

"Who cares about that?" cried Grunty. "I'll think of something. At least we'll get some food — and we don't even have to go shopping! Come on, let's go get ready."

The trolls darted upstairs to get changed. The invitation said that they had to look fancy, but they didn't own any nice clothes.

"I call the bathroom rug as my cloak!" cried Grunty.

"Only if I can have the bedroom lampshade for a hat!" The Grouch hollered.

Chapter 2

The trolls arrived at Sparkleton Elementary at 3:15 p.m. on the dot. They stopped and stared when they saw the long line of well-dressed parents making their way inside.

"Look at their big silly hats!" Grouchy said, giggling to himself.

"Ridiculous!" growled Grunty. "Come on, follow me."

Tummies rumbling loudly, the

trollrific pair made their way across the
playground and got in line. The man in
front of them glanced over his shoulder.
When he saw Grouchy's lampshade hat,
his mouth dropped open in surprise
and he nudged his wife. As she turned
to look, the feather in her hat tickled
Grunty's nose.

"Now look what you've done!" the woman shrieked. "Disgusting!"

"What?" Grunty shrugged. "It was just a sneeze."

Suddenly, a pair of shiny black shoes came squeaking down the line. It was Mr. Spickspan, the principal. He came to a stop in front of the trolls and let out a horrified gasp.

"Not you two!" he said, straightening his already straight tie. Mr. Spickspan still hadn't forgiven the trolls for their last visit when they'd almost wrecked his school. "You two weren't invited! Please leave!"

"If we weren't invited, then what are these?" growled Grunty. He pulled out two crumpled tickets.

"So nah nah nah nah nah!" The Grouch said, sticking out his tongue at the principal.

Mr. Spickspan's left eye gave a nervous twitch. He didn't want a scene.

Not today. There was a reporter coming from the local newspaper. He could see the headline now:

TROLL TROUBLE AT SPARKLETON ELEMENTARY — *AGAIN!*

"Fine!" he hissed. "But I'll be watching you, so don't do anything!"

"As if we would!" The Grunt smiled. "Come on, Grouchy!"

They cut around the line and hurried into the cafeteria.

"Where's the food?" Grunty asked. "I'm starving!"

"I can't see!" Grouchy complained, bouncing up and down. "Grunty, I'm too short! Lift me up!"

Grunty scooped him up and plopped him on top of his head. As The Grunt hurried around searching for the food, Grouchy found himself staring down at all the fancy hats. It was too tempting to just to sit there! Quick as a flash, The Grunt added some finishing touches of his own to the hats — mostly green and slimy touches!

He was almost done when he spotted
a hat with a bunch of shiny cherries
on top. Normally Grouchy didn't eat
cherries — they were way too healthy —
but today he was starving, so he plucked
one off, bit into it, and . . .

"OWWWW!" he yelled. It was a fake!
He tossed the cherry away. It landed
with a *PLOP!* right in Mr. Spickspan's
glass of fruit punch.

"Uh-oh!" Grouchy gasped. The
principal looked furious and he was
headed straight toward them. "Quick,
Grunty, get out of here!"

Grunty whisked Grouchy off his head,
and the trolls took off running through
the crowd. They hadn't gotten very far
when they bumped into Nick and his

friends Julie and Sam, who were busy taking people's coats at the entrance.

"Nick," puffed Grunty, "where's the grub?"

"In the kitchen," Nick whispered. "But you won't like it. It's all healthy and boring, thanks to Mrs. Boil."

"Don't worry about that!" cried Grunty. "Lead us to it!"

Chapter 3

As they reached the kitchen, Grunty skidded to a halt. "Where's Mrs. Boil?" he whispered.

Julie smiled. "You don't need to worry about her," she told them. "She'll be busy serving drinks in the cafeteria all afternoon!"

The trolls looked around the spotless kitchen and gasped in disbelief. It was terrible! There was healthy-looking food covering every available surface. It sat on fancy china plates on top of the shiny countertops.

Grunty shook his head. He'd never seen so many fresh vegetables in his life. "Yuck!" he groaned, untying his cloak and dumping it on the floor. "I might be starving, but I'm not eating that!"

"No way!" Grouchy agreed, tossing

down his lampshade hat. "So what are
we going to do?"

Grunty scratched his head as he
thought. Suddenly, it hit him. "Quick,
everyone, search the cupboards!"
he cried.

LET'S GET STARTED!

The trolls and their friends ran to the cupboards and started pulling open the doors.

"Hang on," said Sam. "What are we supposed to be looking for?"

"Anything to make this food taste better!" cried Grunty.

In no time at all, they'd unearthed a selection of goodies. Ketchup, mustard, vinegar, mayonnaise, and a giant jar of pickled onions were lined up across the table.

Grunty grabbed a bowl of French onion dip off the counter and added it to the pile. "Add some mustard!" he cried excitedly.

He opened the jar of thick yellow mustard and scooped out a huge handful. Then he plopped it into the French onion dip, gave it a nice big stir, then slurped the rest off his hairy fingers. "Delicious!" He grinned. "Okay, what's next?"

One by one, the group turned each boring plate of food into their own "delicious" creation.

Nick spiced up the boring sandwiches with big globs of spicy mustard, while Julie drenched the apples in vinegar. Sam got to work loading the ice cream sundaes with big handfuls of pickled onions.

Grunty smiled. "Good work, everyone!" he said. "Those are going to be a great surprise! Mrs. Boil will be so excited!"

Finally, Grouchy iced the fancy-looking cupcakes Mrs. Boil had made with nice big dollops of ketchup. Then everyone stood back to admire their work.

Grunty's stomach picked that moment to grumble loudly. "I'm sure Mrs. Boil won't mind if we just have a little taste of her 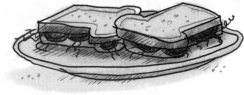 food," he said. He picked up a couple of sandwiches and passed the plate to Grouchy, who immediately stuffed several in his mouth.

"Mmmm!" The Grouch yelled with

his mouth full. "Everyone's going to love this food!"

"Definitely!" Grunty agreed. "It's trollrific!"

Suddenly, Grunty spotted something hidden perched on top of the fridge. "Aha!" he cried, stomping over. "What's this?"

"That's Mrs. Boil's special carrot cake for when the mayor makes her speech," said Julie. "They're going to light those two sparklers on top!"

Grunty's gaze wandered from the carrot cake to a box beside it. On the lid, in big black letters, were the words:

DO NOT TOUCH!

"Hmmm . . ." The Grunt said thoughtfully. He tore the lid off the box, and his eyes grew wide. Inside were hundreds of sparklers!

"These are perfect!" Grunty exclaimed. He grabbed two enormous handfuls of sparklers and stuffed them all into the cake.

He was just finishing up when a group of children burst into the kitchen to collect the food.

"Perfect timing!" said Grunty. "Here it is!"

"There's a special stand for that cake," said Nick. "It's behind the curtain on the stage. I'm in charge of making sure it gets there."

"I'll do that!" Grunty offered with a

big smile. "We don't want anyone seeing it before the big moment or it'll spoil the surprise!"

He scooped up the cake and gazed proudly at the sparklers.

Chapter 4

The trolls hurried out of the kitchen and made their way backstage. Grouchy stood guard as Grunty set the cake on its stand.

"Done," The Grunt whispered. "Now let's eat! I'm starving!"

As the children handed out the delicious snacks they'd created, the trolls grabbed handfuls. They ate and ate, but there was still more food.

Grunty glanced around the room.
Why was nothing running out? he
wondered. As he watched, the mayor
took a bite of one of the fancy-looking
fruit and ketchup cupcakes. She
immediately spit
it back out
and tossed it
behind her.
It landed on
the brim of
someone's
fancy hat.

Grunty
nudged The
Grouch. "How
rude!" he said
with a scowl.

"After all the hard work you put into those cupcakes, she didn't even eat it!"

Some of the parents were complaining too. The trolls couldn't believe their ears! No one liked the food they'd made!

"Urrgh!"one of the fathers said, spitting out his food. "Apples and vinegar — disgusting!"

"Don't touch that dip!" whispered another parent. "It's terrible!"

"Yuck!" Nick's teacher, Mr. Smart, exclaimed. He spit out two pickled onions and stared at his ice cream.

"Here, you'd better have this," growled Grunty, handing him a barf bag. "Just in case."

Mr. Spickspan took a tiny bite of one

of the sandwiches and immediately
started coughing.

"W-water!" he spluttered. He thrust
his head into the bowl of fruit punch
and started lapping it up like a dog.

CLICK! went the reporter's camera!

Mrs. Boil stared in horror. Someone had tampered with all of her healthy snacks! And she knew exactly who was to blame . . . those trolls!

She was about to go give them a piece of her mind when she spotted the mayor making her way toward the stage. It was time for her speech and the unveiling of the cake.

The mayor took her place at the microphone and gave the audience a small smile. She held a napkin over her mouth. She couldn't remember the last time she'd felt so sick! She swallowed hard.

"Ladies and gentlemen," she began. "First of all, I would like to congratulate Sparkleton Elementary on winning healthy food award. It has been a . . . um . . . a lovely party! Mrs. Boil must take all the credit for the disgust — I mean, delicious food,  and I'd like to invite her on to the stage to unveil her . . . um . . . masterpiece."

Still clutching the napkin to her lips, the mayor motioned to Mrs. Boil, who walked toward the stage.

As she made her way toward the microphone, Mrs. Boil looked around nervously. If those trolls had ruined her snacks, there was no telling what had they done to her cake!

Mrs. Boil pulled a cord, and the curtains opened to reveal her carrot cake sitting on the table. At least she thought it was her carrot cake. She hardly recognized it, covered in so many sparklers. It was ruined!

Hands trembling, Mrs. Boil struck a match and lit just one of the hundreds of sparklers.

"Hooray!" Grunty cheered as sparks from the single sparkler began to light the rest.

"Woo-hoo!" Grouchy clapped. "It's glowing like a rocket!"

The trolls grinned happily. But the rest of the crowd didn't seem nearly as excited. In fact, the teachers and parents seemed downright nervous. They were all quickly backing away from the glowing cake. Suddenly . . .

"No!" wailed Mrs. Boil, as sticky
carrot cake rained down on everyone.
"I'll get you trolls for this!"

"Time to go!" cried Grouchy, sprinting
toward the door.

"Wait for me!" Grunty hollered.

The trolls raced past Mr. Spickspan, who had collapsed in a chair, just as the reporter zoomed in for a close-up.

Chapter 1

Whoosh! The Grouch raced into the kitchen and tugged on The Grunt's arm. "Grunty, Grunty!" he hollered. "Do you know what day it is?"

The Grunt looked up from the hair cupcakes he was making and licked the spoon. He stared down at The Grouch, who was clutching a crumpled drawing in his hand. Grunty scratched his head thoughtfully. Then suddenly it came to him — it was Halloween!

Grouchy groaned. He'd forgotten to plan his costume! And judging by the drawing he held, Grouchy had remembered.

"Haha!" Grouch cheered, waving the drawing. "This is my Halloween costume! I'm going to go make it, and then I'll be ready to go trick or treating!"

"Let me see," said Grunty.

"Nope!" The Grouch said with a smile. "You'll just copy it."

He stuffed the drawing under his hat and raced to the pantry. He'd get all the best stuff now — the biggest boogies, the slimiest snot, the jarful of bugs! He knew exactly what he'd need.

"I want that," said The Grunt, sneaking up behind The Grouch and swiping a jar of boogies from his hand.

"Give those back!" yelled Grouchy. "I need them for my costume!"

"Well, so do I!" said The Grunt.

"No, you don't!" cried Grouchy. "You're just a copycat! You don't even know what your costume is yet!"

"Yes, I do!" growled The Grunt. "So there!"

The Grouch grabbed up a bottle of snot, but Grunty swiped it away from him. "I need that too," he growled, "for my costume!"

Grouchy stamped his tiny foot. "You're ruining everything!" He scowled. "How am I supposed to be a boogie monster with an extra-drippy, slimy-snot mustache if you take all the boogies, the snot, and —"

Suddenly, Grouchy stopped. He and Grunty stared at the shelf. The snot was still there for the taking!

In a flash, both trolls grabbed for it, but Grunty got there first.

"Fine!" Grouchy said with a scowl. "Be a meanie then! I'll make a different costume. And it'll be even better. I'm going to be a . . . a were-troll!"

A dreamy look came over Grunty's face. A were-troll — that was brilliant idea! If anyone was cut out to be a were-troll, it was him. Were-trolls were big. Were-trolls were hairy. Were-trolls were mean and

grumpy! Grouchy was just small and green and warty!

"Here," said The Grunt, "have the boogies back. I'm gonna be the were-troll! You can have the bottle of snot back too."

"Okay," said Grouchy, trying his best not to sound too happy. His plan to trick The Grunt had worked! Now he could be the boogie monster, just like he'd planned, except . . .

"Can I have the hairballs too?" Grouchy asked politely. "I need them for my mustache."

"No way!" The Grunt snapped. "I need them for my hairy were-troll costume!"

He thundered away, clutching the

jar of hairballs. He needed every single strand. In fact, now that he thought about it, one measly jar of hair wasn't going to make a whole were-troll costume! He'd have to go on a hair-hunt. But where should he start?

Chapter 2

Two hours later, Grunty stomped into the bathroom. He'd searched everywhere and still didn't have enough hair to make his were-troll costume.

The Grunt climbed into the filthy bathtub, stuck his fingers down the drain, and wiggled them around. There was something down there! Carefully, Grunty pulled his fingers back out.

"Shoot!" he roared, as a fat, hairy spider wriggled between his fingers.

He heaved himself up and was about
to climb out of the tub when something
burst through the door. It looked like a
big, slimy pea wearing a hat.

"Rahhhhh!" The Grouch yelled. "The
boogie monster's coming to get you!"

Grunty sighed.

"What's wrong?" asked Grouchy. "Where's your costume?"

"I can't find enough hair!" Grunty said. "I can't go trick-or-treating tonight without a costume."

Grouchy looked sad. "But we always go together!" he said. "There has to be somewhere we can get some hair."

Suddenly he had an idea. "Wait!" he cried. "How about the hairdresser's?"

"Great idea!" Grunty said. "There are always piles on the floor! What are we waiting for? Let's go!"

The trolls raced downstairs. As they ran past the kitchen, Grunty paused. "Hang on," he said, grabbing a dirty pan out of the sink. "We can collect the hair in this!"

With that, the trolls darted out of the house. "Hurry up or we'll miss the bus!" Grunty cried.

"I can't!" puffed The Grouch. "It's this snot! I'm sticking to the pavement!"

The bus was about to pull away from the curb as the trolls leaped aboard.

"Hold on," said the bus driver, scowling at Grouchy. "No slimy things are allowed on my seats."

The Grouch beamed. "I'm a boogie mon—"

"He'll sit on my lap!" Grunty cut in. He scooped up Grouchy and dove for a seat.

With a sigh, the bus driver pulled away. Grouchy smiled. Sitting up on Grunty's lap meant he could see for once! He and Grunty spent the whole journey secretly flicking snot at the other passengers.

Fifteen minutes later, the bus came to a stop right outside Claude's, the fanciest hairdressing salon in town.

"I like being a boogie monster!" Grouchy said as they stepped off the bus. He flicked some snot at a woman walking past. "It's fun!"

Grunty peered through the salon window. It looked very fancy. "Yuck," he groaned. "It's horrible."

"Disgusting!" Grouchy agreed.

A woman was sipping tea as a hairdresser cut her hair. He jumped in surprise when he saw two snotty noses pressed against the glass.

SNIP! went his shiny scissors before he could stop them. A huge chunk of the woman's hair tumbled to the floor. Grunty's eyes lit up. He'd take that piece!

"Come on!" he cried, hurrying to the door. As he pushed it open, he noticed a sign on the glass.

Feeling blue?
Need a free hairdo?

Let Claude work his magic on you!
Models needed **NOW!**

"They can forget about that!" growled The Grunt as he stomped into the salon. "Nobody's touching my hair!"

Chapter 3

The hairdresser left the woman drinking her tea and hurried across the salon to the trolls. He smiled at his reflection in a mirror as he passed.

"Good afternoon, gentlemen," he said, pushing a long, silky piece of hair off his forehead. "I am Claude, hairdresser to the stars! How can I hel—" Suddenly, Claude stopped and stared at the trolls. One of them was covered in slime.

He quickly snatched up a newspaper and set it on the floor near The Grouch. "Would you mind standing on this?" he asked.

Grouchy squelched forward and stood on it.

"There!" Claude said, sounding relieved. "That's better! My goodness, you two do need my magic, don't you?"

"No!" snapped The Grunt. "We don't need our hair done, if that's what you mean!"

"We just need some hair!" Grouchy added. He dropped to his knees and started scooping up hair from the floor. It stuck to his hands, which were still covered in snot.

The entire salon watched in horror. If

anyone needed a makeover, it was these
two!

"Hold on a minute!" Claude said.
"You can't just take that hair. No, no, no!
I need models, and you two are perfect.
There's so much I could do to you! Then,
when I've worked my magic, you can
have as much hair as you like!"

Grouchy shot off the floor and hid behind The Grunt. "Quick, let's get out of here," he whispered. "I don't want to be a —"

"Not so fast," hissed Grunty, pulling The Grouch aside. "If we leave now, I won't have a costume! I thought you wanted me to go trick or treating tonight!"

"I do," Grouchy said. "But I'm not being a model! They'll wash my boogie man costume right down the drain!"

Grunty sighed. Grouchy was right. And that meant one thing — he'd have to be Claude's model!

"Fine," he whispered, leaning closer to The Grouch. "Listen up. I've got a plan. . . ."

When Grunty had finished whispering his plan, Grouchy looked confused. "So you'll get all prettied up," he said, "and while Claude's working his magic, I'll swipe hair off the floor?"

"No!" hissed Grunty. "I *don't* get prettied up! That's the whole point. I'll

keep Claude talking about what he's planning to do, and you creep around collecting hair. Then we'll sneak out of here before he gets started. Got it?"

"Uh . . . got it!" said Grouchy. "I think."

Grunty turned back to Claude. "All right," he growled. "I'll be your model!"

"Perfect!" cried Claude, clapping his hands. "Let me just finish up with my client first."

"Fine," said Grunty, "but I've got tons of questions to ask before you touch my hair."

"Of course!" Claude said with a smile. He led The Grunt toward the sparkly mirrors, helped him into a long black cape, and settled him in a chair.

Meanwhile, Grouchy sat himself down in the waiting area. It wasn't time to swipe the hair yet. Grunty had told him to wait until Claude was busy chatting.

He picked up a magazine to look at while he waited. As he did, something fell to the floor. He snatched it up, and his eyes grew wide. It was the latest edition of his favorite comic!

"Wow!" he gasped, making himself comfy.

Chapter 4

In no time at all, Claude had finished with his first client and turned his attention to The Grunt.

"Your turn!" Claude said cheerfully.

Grunty gulped. He could see The Grouch in the mirror, and he didn't seem to be paying much attention. What if he didn't remember the plan?

"Tell me what you're going to do first," growled Grunty. "Everything . . ."

Claude smiled and started running his fingers through Grunty's knotty hair. "This could take a while," he sighed, shaking his head.

The Grunt squirmed as Claude started to rattle off a list of what he had planned — washing, cutting, dyeing, drying, curling, fluffing-up. It sounded like torture!

Claude went on and on. The salon was hot and stuffy. *Buzzzzzz!* went the hairdryers. *Ssssshhhh!* went the water in the sinks. On and on and on . . .

Soon, Grunty's eyes began to feel heavy. Then, very slowly . . . they closed.

Meanwhile, Grouchy was in the middle of an awesome *Splat Bat* comic. The Vampire Splat Bats had teamed up with the Boogie Monster! Captain Sparkle had no chance now!

The minutes flew by as Grouchy read on and on. Just one more story . . . then another one. Suddenly, The Grouch heard a familiar sound.

Zzzzz . . . zzzzz . . .

Grouchy froze. Was that Grunty snoring? No, it couldn't be! How could he be asleep? He'd only sat down a minute ago. Hadn't he?

Grouchy looked up and checked the clock on the wall. Five o'clock! That meant he'd been reading for more than an hour!

The Grouch quickly tossed away the comic and threw himself on to the floor. He needed hair, right now! Then he'd have to rescue Grunty before Claude started working his magic!

He scrambled around, scooping up hair. There was tons of it on the floor. Tons and tons of . . . purple hair.

Trembling, Grouchy climbed to his feet and peered up at Grunty where he sat snoring in the salon chair.

"Uh-oh!" Grouchy whispered. It seemed that while he'd been busy reading his comic, Claude had already worked his magic.

UH-OH!

Grunty's normally purple hair was
now black and fluffy. A thick white
stripe ran straight down the middle,
making The Grouch look like a skunk!

Grouchy gulped. Grunty was going to be furious with him. He'd ruined the whole plan.

"Grunty! Wake up!" The Grouch yelled, waving his arms at the sleeping troll.

"Excuse me!" Claude snapped, sounding irritated. "I'm not finished yet!"

Grouchy ignored him and gave The Grunt a sharp bite on the ankle. Suddenly, Grunty began to stir.

Quick as a flash, Grouchy swiveled Grunty's chair around so that he had his back to the mirror. If he saw himself now there'd be big trouble!

"What the . . . what's going on?" Grunty asked, rubbing his eyes.

"RUN!" yelled Grouchy. He grabbed Grunty's arm and tugged him toward the door.

The rest of the customers in the salon gasped as the trollrific pair thundered past them. Some of the customers even jumped out of their chairs and sprinted out of the salon.

"Did you get the hair?" Grunty asked when they got outside. But Grouchy just kept on running.

"Uh . . . a bit," The Grouch puffed as he ran.

Then, suddenly . . .

"Arrgghhh!" a woman on the street screamed. She pointed at The Grunt in terror.

The street cleared in seconds. What was going on?

Puzzled, Grunty looked down at himself. He was still wearing the long black cape Claude had given him, but it couldn't be that, could it? He reached up and felt his hair. His hair! What had Claude done?

The Grunt thundered across the

street to a store window and peered at his reflection. His jaw dropped — he looked like a giant skunk! It was wicked! And it was super-scary!

Just then, the moon began to shine. It was time to go trick or treating!

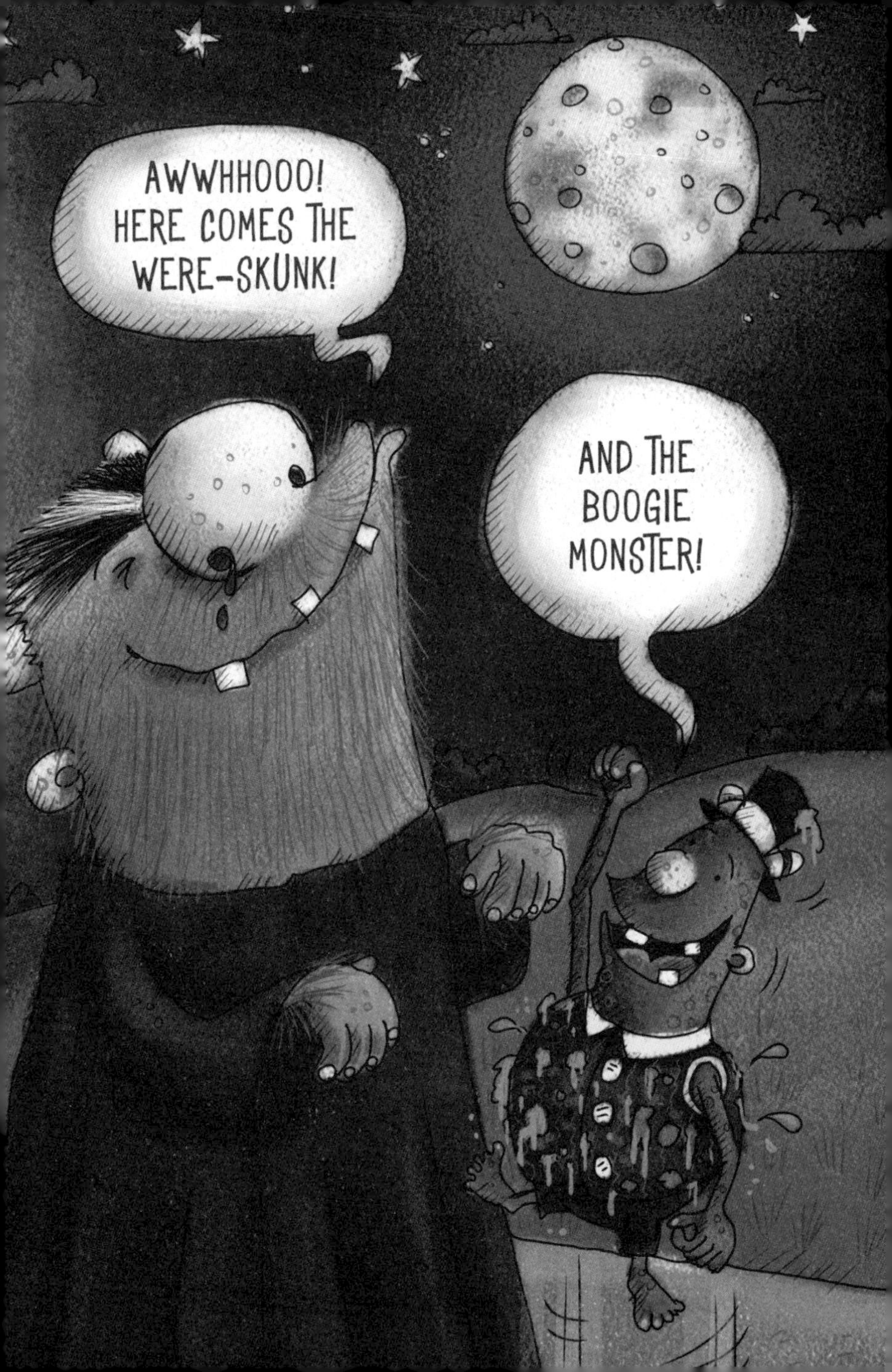
AWWHHOOO! HERE COMES THE WERE-SKUNK!
AND THE BOOGIE MONSTER!

Chapter 1

"Move!" cried Grunty, poking at his snail. But Snail didn't even twitch!

The trolls were in the garden, racing their pets, but so far they'd barely even moved.

"That makes Slug the winner!" Grouchy exclaimed with a grin.

Grunty peered down at Slug. "How come? He hasn't moved either!"

"Yes, he has!" Grouchy insisted, pointing out an almost-invisible slithery trail. "See! Right there! So hand over my boogie winnings!"

Grunty shook his head and clutched the boogie jar. "These pets are useless!" he roared. "They don't do anything!"

The Grunt picked up a stick and threw it across the yard. "Fetch, Snail!" he commanded.

Snail didn't budge. Grunty picked him up and peered into his shell.

"Now where did you go?" The Grunt bellowed. He shook his head and sighed. "Grouchy, I think it's time we got a new pet."

Grouchy let out a horrified gasp and covered Slug's ears. (He wasn't sure if Slug had ears, so he just covered where ears would be if he had any.)

"Don't say that!" he whispered. "You'll upset him!"

But even Grouchy had to admit that Slug was a little boring. He didn't have fleas. He didn't chase the mailman. He didn't chew holes in the curtains. And he hardly ever burped out loud!

For the next half an hour, Grunty and Grouchy sat side by side in the mud, arguing about whether they should get a new pet or not. Eventually, they decided that they would.

"Okay," growled The Grunt. "Now that it's settled, what pet should we get?"

"Something with fleas!" cried Grouchy. "And something that has tons of hair and loves mud and garbage!"

"Hmmm," said Grunty thoughtfully. "Like what?"

"I know!" cried Grouchy. "Let's get a gorilla!" He puffed out his cheeks and beat his chest as he made monkey noises.

"A gorilla would eat us out of house and home!" Grunty said. "We need something smaller. How about a bat? It would fly all over the house and make a trollrific mess!"

"Bats sleep all day!" Grouchy said. "That's no good." He scratched his head. Choosing a pet was harder than he'd thought.

"What about a giraffe!" cried Grouchy.

"Or a toad!" cried Grunty.

"Orangutan!"

"Warthog!"

"Hippopotamus!"

On and on the trolls argued. They

couldn't come to an agreement. Finally, Grunty had a great idea.

"Why don't we go to the pet shop?" he said. "Maybe we'll find something there we both like."

"Good idea!" cried Grouchy excitedly.

Leaving Slug and Snail to entertain themselves, the trolls raced to the bus stop. On the way, they talked about what pets they might find in the pet shop.

By the time they arrived, they'd decided what they wanted. They couldn't believe they hadn't thought of it before!

"Good morning!" called Grouchy, as they hurried into the pet shop.

The store clerk backed up nervously at the sight of the trolls. He didn't want them bringing fleas into his shop!

"We're looking for a new pet," The Grunt growled.

Chapter 2

"Wh-what?" the pet-shop man stuttered. He looked horrified. "You want a smelly rat? But all my rats are clean! And very smart!"

"Huh! Well, that's no good!" The Grunt complained. "What else do you have?"

"Anything with fangs that burps a lot?" asked Grouchy.

"How about a rabbit?" the man suggested. "They're so sweet!" He opened the door of the rabbit pen and the trolls peered inside.

"Yuck!" Grouchy hollered, jumping back from the cage in horror.

"They're fluffy!" Grunty said with a disgusted shudder.

The man shut the door to the cage, and the trolls turned to look around the shop. All these pets looked way too clean! None of them were even scratching!

"They all look bored," Grunty said. "You should let them play together."

"NO!" the pet-shop man yelled, as The Grunt opened the rabbit cage. A herd of fluffy bunnies immediately hopped out. The pet-store man tried to catch them, but they were just too fast!

Meanwhile, Grouchy opened the birdcage. "Tada!" he said as the birds flew out into the shop.

"Now for those clean rats!" cried Grunty, opening the rats' cage.

"Noooo!" wailed the pet-store man.

"They'll . . . they'll . . . get dirty!" But
it was too late. The rats were out and
scurrying across the floor.

SPLAT! SPLAT! SPLAT! Parrot poop
rained down, landing on the other
animals.

"GET OUT!" the man yelled. "NOW!"

"You should really get some more interesting pets!" Grouchy yelled as the trolls made their way to the door.

"With fleas!" added Grunty. He slammed the door shut behind him.

Out on the sidewalk, Grouchy looked upset. He'd been sure they'd find a nice

new pet in there. "What are we going to do now?" he said.

But, for once, Grunty didn't have an answer.

The trolls wandered back through the park, and Grunty jumped in all the muddy puddles along the way. But try as he might, he couldn't cheer Grouchy up.

"Look, there's an ice-cream truck," said Grunty, hurrying over. "You love ice cream! You wait here. I'll even ask if they have boogie sprinkles!"

Grouchy flopped down under a big tree and let out a sigh. He'd been so excited about getting a new pet.

As he waited, a scruffy dog appeared. He was big and brown and as hairy as a woolly mammoth! He sniffed

the tree where Grouchy sat.
Then he sniffed The Grouch.
He seemed to like Grouchy's smell,
because he didn't run away. Instead,
he flopped down next to Grouchy and
scratched.

"Wow!" cried Grouchy. "You've got
fleas!"

The dog started to pant. His breath
smelled like stinky pond water!

"Here you go, Grouchy!" The Grunt
said, stomping back with two
ice cream cones. The fleabag

dog jumped up and snatched one out of right out of Grunty's hand.

"Hey!" cried Grunty, snatching it back.

"Never mind!" The Grouch said with a giggle. "He's got fleas, stinky breath, he's naughty, and it looks like he doesn't have a home. I found our perfect pet!"

Chapter 3

Over the next few weeks, the scruffy dog, which Grouchy named Fleabag, proved to be the best pet in the world.

Fleabag slurped. Fleabag burped. Fleabag barked at the mailman. Fleabag chewed huge holes in the curtains and rolled in the mud every chance he got.

Another one of Fleabag's special talents was drooling. In just three weeks, the trolls had managed to collect seven jars of drool. Their pantry had never held so many treats!

Everyone was happy until one sunny afternoon, when everything changed. The trolls and Fleabag were out in town when Fleabag came nose to nose with the most beautiful dog in the world!

She had a curly white coat and a tail like a snowball on a stick. Fleabag had never seen anything so lovely.

As the dog trotted out of the Pampered Pooch Salon, she bumped right into Fleabag, who was munching on some stale bread.

"Oh, goodness!" her owner exclaimed. "What a disgusting dog!" The woman gripped the poodle's sparkly leash and squeezed past the trolls. "Don't look at them, Fifi-Belle, darling!"

Fleabag stared at the pretty poodle. His drool-covered jaw dropped. A warm, fuzzy look crept into his eyes.

Grunty and Grouchy stared at each other. What was wrong with their dog?

As Fifi-Belle pranced away, Fleabag scrambled to his feet and raced after her. Fleabag was in love!

"No!" yelled Grouchy, racing after

him. But Fleabag was already at Fifi-Belle's side, panting madly.

"Eww!" cried her owner. "What smelly breath! Get him away!"

Grunty thundered up behind them and scooped Fleabag into his arms.

"Come on, we're going home!" he
roared.

As the trolls stomped away, Fleabag
noticed that Fifi-Belle was heading
to the park. Maybe he'd see her there
tomorrow. . . .

For the rest of
the day, Fleabag
whimpered and
whined. He lay
in his basket and
wouldn't eat or play.

That night, the trolls went to bed
feeling very worried. They'd never seen
Fleabag like this before. What was the
matter with him?

The next morning, Grouchy jumped out of bed and immediately looked around for Fleabag.

"Where is he?" he gasped. "He's normally chewing a bone on my bed!"

They checked the garden. There were no new holes. They checked the curtains. There were no new holes. Where on earth was Fleabag, and what was he up to?

"Don't worry," said Grunty. "We'll go search around town. He probably went back to the dumpsters! Come on!"

As they hurried out of the door, Grouchy spotted something. There was a dog by their gate.

"Look!" he gasped. "It's . . . wait . . . oh, never mind. It isn't him."

There was no way this dog was
Fleabag. This dog looked too clean and
neat. It couldn't be!

"Scram!" yelled Grunty. "Go on!
Grrr!" But the dog came trotting toward
them.

The trolls stared in disbelief. It *was*
Fleabag! But his fur was short and shiny,
and he smelled clean.

The trolls shuddered in disgust. He must have gone to the Pampered Pooch Salon to make himself look and smell this bad.

"Quick!" whispered Grunty. "Get him inside before anyone sees him!"

"Or smells him," Grouchy said. "Bad dog, Fleabag!"

Chapter 4

For the rest of the morning, Fleabag paced around the house, pawing the front door. His eyes were sad, and his clean tail drooped.

"What does he want?" The Grunt growled.

Grouchy shrugged. "How am I supposed to know?"

They offered him boogie snacks. They offered him bones. They offered him boogies on bones! But Fleabag just kept pawing at the front door and whining sadly.

Finally, Grouchy got the message. "Hang on," he said. "I think he wants to go on a walk!"

Fleabag's ears pricked up at once, and his tail started wagging happily. That was it! He wanted to go on a walk to the park.

"Well, I'm not taking him anywhere looking like that!" Grunty growled. "I want the old Fleabag back!"

The trolls tried everything to persuade Fleabag to get dirty. Drippy ice cream, a muddy bath . . . they even offered to have a food fight! But Fleabag turned his clean nose up at everything.

"He'll have to wear a disguise then," sighed Grunty. "Or no walk!" He pulled out an old sweater and hat, which Grouchy helped Fleabag put on.

Fleabag sniffed the sweater and whimpered. It stunk, and he didn't want to stink! Not today.

On the way to the park, Fleabag trotted by Grunty's side and carefully stepped around all the mud puddles.

"What is wrong with that dog?" The Grunt snapped. "I wish he was like he used to be."

By the time they made it to the park it was raining. Fleabag quickly hurried under a tree to stay dry. And there he sat, peering around, for what seemed like hours.

Then, suddenly, Fleabag perked up. He wriggled out of The Grunt's old sweater, shook off the hat, and raced across the park toward . . .

"Fifi-Belle!" The Grunt exclaimed with a scowl. "So that's why he went to that pampered pooch place! Fleabag's trying to impress that poodle!"

The trolls watched in horror as Fleabag trotted up to Fifi-Belle's owner and held out a spotlessly clean paw for her to shake.

They stared as the woman took it and

patted him gently on the head. Clearly, she didn't recognize Fleabag from yesterday!

Then they watched in horror as Fleabag and Fifi-Belle began to play with a ball. Not chew it up. Not drool on it — just play.

"I've had enough of this!" The Grunt growled angrily. "Come on, let's go get him!"

"No, wait a second!" said Grouchy. He'd spotted something that might solve their problem for them. "Look over there."

As The Grunt and The Grouch watched, a fancy black poodle came trotting along the path. He stopped right in front of Fifi-Belle and Fleabag.

Fifi-Belle gazed up at him and let out a yappy little bark. The black poodle barked back at her. Fifi-Belle's little snowball tail began to wag. It was love at first bark!

The two poodles trotted away through the trees together, their owners strolling behind. Fleabag hung his head and whimpered.

"It's okay, Fleabag!" cried Grouchy,

dashing over and giving him a hug.
"Forget Fifi-Belle. We love you, boy!"

The Grunt quickly hurried off and
bought three ice cream cones. He placed
them on the grass in front of Fleabag.

After a while, Fleabag licked one. Then he slurped them up, one after the other, and finished with a giant burp.

"That's more like it!" said Grunty. "He's back to normal. Let's go home!"

They stomped off under the trees and through the flowerbeds. Then, as they reached the park gates, they found a ginormous mud puddle!

"Whee!" cried the trolls, jumping in. "We love mud puddles!"

"Woof!" barked Fleabag, joining them. He couldn't have agreed more!

Tracey Corderoy

was born and grew up in South Wales before moving to Bath, England to become a teacher. Tracey has always been passionate about writing for children and convinced that language, expressed through wonderful literature, is the key to stimulating learning and imagination. She currently lives in an ancient cottage with her husband, two daughters, and their many animals.

Lee Wildish

lives in Lancashire, England and has been drawing since a very young age. He loves illustrating children's books and thinks there's nothing better than seeing people laughing at a book he's illustrated.

READ MORE ABOUT **THE GRUNT AND THE GROUCH** AT capstonekids.com/characters/grunt-grouch